Angelina's Island

Jeanette Winter

Frances Foster Books
Farrar, Straus and Giroux • New York

Copyright © 2007 by Jeanette Winter
All rights reserved
Distributed in Canada by Douglas & McIntyre Ltd.
Color separations by Chroma Graphics PTE Ltd.
Printed and bound in China
Designed by Jeanette Winter and Symon Chow
First edition, 2007
1 3 5 7 9 10 8 6 4 2

www.fsgkidsbooks.com

Library of Congress Cataloging-in-Publication Data
Winter, Jeanette.
    Angelina's island / Jeanette Winter.— 1st ed.
        p. cm.
    Summary: Every day, Angelina dreams of her home in Jamaica and imagines she
is there, until her mother finds a wonderful way to convince her that New York
is now their home.
    ISBN-13: 978-0-374-30349-5
    ISBN-10: 0-374-30349-5
    [1. Homesickness—Fiction. 2. Jamaican Americans—Fiction. 3. Parades—Fiction.
4. Jamaica—Fiction. 5. New York (N.Y.)—Fiction.] I. Title.
PZ7.W7547 Ang 2007
[E]—dc22
                                                                                            2005052752

To the children of New York City
who dance in the West Indian Day Parade

Every day I tell Mama,
I want to go home.
Every day she tells me,
We are home, Angelina.
New York is home now.

But this is not home—
it doesn't sound like home,
it doesn't look like home,
it doesn't feel like home.

Every night I dream
of my island in the sun.

I dream that the airplane that brought me here
is taking me back home to Jamaica.
I don't want to wake up
and leave my sunny dreams.

Every morning I tell Mama,
I want to go home.
Every morning she tells me,
We are home, Angelina.
Eat your breakfast.
But I want my island food.

I dream about mangos, guavas, papayas,
green bananas, star apples, breadfruit,
callaloo, chocho, johnnycake, sugarcane,
ackee, and salt fish.
And I wake up hungry.

The tall buildings hide
the sun and the sky.

In my dreams the sun warms my head,
and the sand warms my feet,
and the sky is always blue.

I want this bus I ride to school
to take me back home.

I close my eyes and feel my toes
in the dust of a dirt road,
walking to my island school.
The bus stops and I open my eyes
to the cold city.

The bird on my window ledge has gray feathers.
Would his feathers turn red and yellow and green
under the Jamaica sun?

I close my eyes and fly home.
Rainbow-colored birds surround me.
But when I open my eyes
the gray bird still sits on the ledge.

Mama and Papa tell me
we have a better life here.
But I miss Mama all day while she works.
I miss Papa all night while he works.

And I miss my grandma all the time.
I talk to her in my dreams.

I don't know the new games here.
I want to play the old games
I know from Jamaica.

I close my eyes and remember
dancing at Carnival with my friends,
our costumes glowing like fire.

Then one day Mama sees something
in the newspaper.
Angelina will like this, she says to herself.

Angelina is missing home, she tells some ladies.
Can she join in the parade?
Yes, of course, but definitely, the ladies answer.
I still want to go home, I tell Mama.
Just wait, she tells me.

Mama takes me to the costume place.
The ladies measure me.
Your costume must fit just so, they say.

I see ladies cutting cloth.
You will glow like the sun, they say.

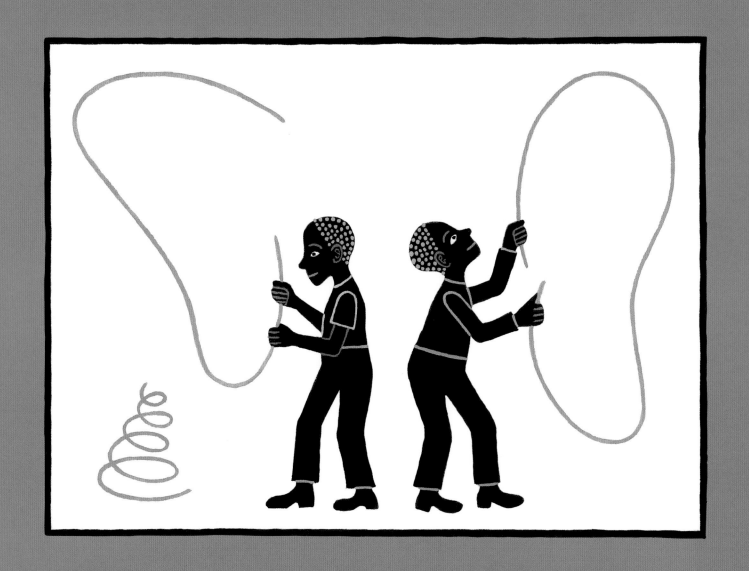

I see men bending wire.
We are making your wings, they say.

I see ladies sewing shiny beads on the cloth.
You will shine like the stars, they say.

Every day I practice dancing for the parade.
I tell Mama, I still want to go home.
Just wait, she says.

At last Carnival day is here.
Mama sprinkles glitter on my face.
The music begins—
this sounds like home!

This looks like home!

This feels like home!

I'm home, Mama.

This is my island in the sun.

Author's Note

Every year on Labor Day, Carnival takes place in Brooklyn, New York. The tradition has come a long way, from Africa to the Caribbean Islands to the streets of New York. Mas bands, steel drum music, reggae, calypso, and food stalls all intertwine at Carnival. A mas band is a parade of masqueraders, dressed in elaborate costumes around a central theme. There may be many people in a band, or just a few. A storefront is usually rented in which to design and construct and sew the costumes. It often takes a whole year to make them. West Indian children have their own mas bands and parade on the Saturday before Labor Day, with costumes as elaborate as those of the adults. After they parade down city streets, a grand finale and dance competition is held on a stage before thousands of people. Carnival keeps alive the traditions of the West Indian people and their ancestors.